AuthorHouse™
1663 Liberty Drive
Bloomington, IN 47403
www.authorhouse.com
Phone: 1 (800) 839-8640

Published by AuthorHouse 8/24/2015

ISBN: 978-1-5049-3313-1 (sc)
978-1-5049-3314-8 (e)

Print information available on the last page.

This book is printed on acid-free paper.

A College Musical

Written By;

Silver A. Lee

Give Me "Ann Answer"

I don't know why I feel this way but I've, been waiting for so long for this day. It feels like all I believed in is wrong but, I won't let know one change my personality! No way... you live only one always get necessities. Don't let know one put you down talking about you ain't nobody, don't have pre-marital sex, always keep yourself on deck.

Indeed, indeed...

You are not alone sometimes I feel the same way you do. You are not alone because, I am a parent too.

Don't ignore me.

Don't ignore me..

Can anybody here me?

Can anybody here me?

Give me answer!

Give me Ann Answer...

Can anybody here me?

Don't you ignore me

Give me answer...

"You I was missing"

It was you I was missing you I was kissing before I was dissing know you tripping. Baby, listen out of all women why you gotta, gotta do this to me? Save the drama, I don't want to fall in love, I don't wanna fall in love with again. Sweet love spending time promises never kept probably was not even mine. You played games with me, and you were always lying to me. You never answer my calls what's up with that?

What's up with that? I don't want to play these games with you I don't wanna be your fool. " I don't care what you like". I don't care what you do out of spite all I know, is that I love you, and from this moment on

I will stay strong. I still love you baby.. Empress Ann

Preface

After the first, second, and third relationship. I decided to just move on with my life. I'm sick, and tired of the same so called I love you's.

Yeah, I know you love me but, it's not like you are going to do what you said. I have heard that before, and I have had plenty of sex to last me a lifetime. Thanks to men like you portraying themselves as husband material. I hate it when guys say something that they do not mean. And, I know because; it happen to me. I might as well say I am use to guys tossing me around as if I were a football. Even Army men.

But, who cares? Right? Out of every date that I had ever had it never fails about how I feel about him. I already know what he want's like every man does, that never fails within itself. Except for this one guy I dated, it seem like we was never together, it seem like he was always there, but then he never was. I never new how I could feel about him.

I didn't know I was going to love him when I got older. I was under the impression that he loved someone else. I was under the impression that I was nobody to him.

But, as the months went by I kind of felt his spirit it felt kind, sweet, for some odd reason concern but, not much of a helper. Sad to say during the mid twenties of my life, it was either happiness, going away, or killing myself. After all then I didn't have to put up with people trying to control me. I didn't have to deal with being in or out of love, nor giving my love away. Either because, I wanted to or because of feelings. Why love? Because, in the end he never cared, he never did in the first place. All he cared about was having sex. I didn't believe that he loved me. Sometimes, it's hard to see who is the leader, and who is the follower. Even though, it took years for Hilary to be with Jirah she felt that her love for him, that he just would not understand how she honestly felt.

"I want to be in love.

I want to feel love.

I want to be in love with a wonderful feeling. Not sad, not hurtful, nor pain. I want to feel just right". By the time she became older Hilary had know ides that she'd actually be with Jirah.

"You are the most beautiful woman I have ever seen". Said Jirah.

"I know all you want is sex". Said Hilary to Jirah.

Chapter One

Yummy, this is good but, I got to go. " I'll be late for school, my first class is my favorite". Said, Hilary. I'll be home between two, and four o'clock; "while walking out the door and closing the door behind her. A young girl growing into a woman, Hilary is such a unique young lady, she has really healthy, pretty length hair, color like the earth brown, and light brown hazel eyes. She is a perfect height, and perfect weight.

Hilary is really pretty.

While waiting for the bus she wonder what her boyfriend was doing. Most likely he was doing the same thing but, Hilary still could not understand why hasn't he called her. " Finally, the bus" Hilary say's to herself. " that will be eighty cents one way,and one dollar for an all day pass." The bus driver had explained. " I'll need an all day pass." bus pass please", Hilary said to the driver. " Thank You" in reply. Hilary held on to the pole walking her way to sit down in a seat. While sitting on the bus passing by the stores, and the gas stations. Watching other people get on to the bus, and off the bus. It takes a couple buses in order to get to the college.

Besides, going to school their was not much to do but, take care of herself, and clean up at home. " hey. Miss lady, how are you doing? With your pretty self." A man had asked Hilary. In turn she said, I'm fine. And as she turn around he said. " I am good, I am okay thank you." I got to go this is my stop, said Hilary. " You got a man"? The guy asked. " yes...yes, I do as a matter fact I am married." Hilary told him as she rolled her eyes. The guy started to laugh, ha-ha and you still ridding the bus? Baby, as long as you are with him you will never know what real love is about, let alone what it is like. How a man suppose to treat the woman he loves". She had given him a blank look "shut up" Hilary mumbled as she existed the bus. " au, just in time Hilary thought the next bus, pulled up back to back. " thank you, and have a nice day" the bus driver said." Are you going to be here for a few minutes? Hilary asked. No, probably the next bus stop," he answered. Oh, okay dang, I am going to be a few minutes late. Arriving at the college Hilary rushed off the bus going to her Anatomy class. Page one- twenty five, class today we will be learning about bone structure. Also I'm giving all of you a pop quiz, I hope you've all studied the chapters I have assigned you to study last week. Remember, these quizzes that I give you is not part of your grade, instead it is points that will help you pass this class, and your final. Ahhh..

Charles, Hilary, and Woo, will you be here on campus tomorrow? Asked the Professor. Yes, I'm here everyday except for Fridays. Said Hilary. Me too, said Charles. I have Football practice on Friday's. I'll be here if I need to be", said Woo. I was going to have the three of you do your quizzes in my office but, instead come to class on Friday, let's say about ten thirtyish? Cool, okay, ah sound good practice isn't till noon anyway. Hilary, Woo, and Charles had said. Great... It is settled, but in the mean time study because, it is vital that you pass all test, and quizzes, said themselves Professor. " oh my god! Am I failing?" asked Hilary. Awww.. man what am I gone do now? Said woo. No! Their goes my career, said Charles. The entire class laughed hysterically. So did the professor, no, no you guys are not failing. It's just that I know you three are athletes and you know like I know how important it is to keep your grades up.

So you won't get kicked off the team, explained their teacher. Oh, replied Hilary; that is such a good idea, yeah said Charles, and woo. So, excitedly why do we have to wait? Anyway? Hilary asked. You need to get a good grade this chapter, I mean chapters are pretty intense.

Professor said. " sudden silence, and everyone was taking the quiz and studying for the quiz on Friday. A, Hilary said Charles. How is your relationship going? It's going; answered, Hilary. I haven't heard from him in a few days, I was thinking that he was busy working and studying for college, you know same as me". You mean he has not called you at all? Asked Charles. Um, Woo you have a first name? Asked Hilary. Your getting of the subject, yes, it's Kim my name is Kim Woo. That is a pretty name. And, to answer you guys question, no he has not called me but, I'm pretty sure he'll come by this weekend besides we want to have a beautiful life together when we get older. Graduate from college get a great job, nice car, beautiful home; you know happily ever after type life style. Explained Hilary. Yeah but, is he the reason why you hardly study? Because, your always thinking of him, when he could care less about you, said Woo. "What, you are" said Hilary. I'm kidding. Says woo. And Hilary said, " I was going to say mean ". But, your probably right he is never home when I go by; I be like is Jirah home? No, he's not his father always say's. Then when I do get to see him he is always in his dumb SUV smoking, seriously never fails he act like he has an internal, eternal disease. Replied Hilary. Hum, we see and how do that make you feel? Said Charles yeah, how? Said Woo.

Nothing, I guess I really do not have time for him but, I make time for him. Hilary had said to woo. Have you had sex? Woo asked., Nowa!

Said Hilary. Maybe he has another girlfriend, Charles said. Hum" shrugging her shoulders. Maybe he does. I'm just saying Hilary a heart can only take so many heart breaks". It is not your fault that he approached you, while you was minding you own business". Your not going to get over him over night, added woo. Woo, we're still together. Well if he got a girl already, just the way it seems, he does not seem worth it. It sounds like you are wasting your time, let me know if I was right look me up.

Said woo.. your such a smart foreigner, said Hilary. I think so to but, I'm just hopping that I am wrong. You know giving it a benefit of a doubt.

Said Hilary. I really like him, " sighing" I don't know what to do I am not happy to admit this but, I fell in love, and I am not happy. Especially having these thoughts about him with another woman. Explained Hilary.

Well, if you two are up for a group study at the library text, or email, said Charles. I'm out. Class is dismissed! Shouted the professor, and you three Hilary, Charles, and Kim do not forget Friday. " alright, no prob pro see you all latter, and have a nice day said Hilary. I will, I will indeed do that, with a smile said, the professor.

A! A! Hilary say's woo. As Hilary turn around yes, woo, why are you looking at me like that? Asked Hilary. Your so pretty, I'm sorry about your relationship, I

was thinking how about you, and me? We can go out sometime? As friends say's woo. We're classmates, and your international I like you as a school mate I would not want to make the relationship odd than what it already is. Wait that didn't come out right. I'm a girl, your a boy accidents happen.
Sex, and kissing stirring into each other, we're unsupervised. I just hate myself if I was ever. " I ain't sweating you baby", it was only a question of concern. When you get ready don't be afraid to let me know, I would like to get to know you; what class you have next? Said woo.
" Demanding", I think I have either math, or speech. Um, um, um, no, no I have swimming." said Hilary. " know, Woo; Kim woo is not the Asian type you would see everyday. Kim woo has pretty brown eyes, his voice is pretty deep. However, his deep voice matches his height, he is pretty attractive." what are your plans after school? Asked woo. Smiling, and feeling shy, Hilary replied", I was thinking about going over to my grandmother's house, you know go hang out with grandma for awhile, help her clean most likely do the yard, you know be a grandchild loving old stories. Said Hilary. Alright, well I'll see you tomorrow, don't forget about the test around ten-thirtyish. Woo said to Hilary as he smiled at her. Okay, Kim see you. " while walking away going to the gym. Since Hilary had

not put on her swim suit under her clothes at home she had to go to her locker. " hum, I wonder if Elkiss came to school today? Hello, Hilary how are you doing this afternoon? Life treating you good? Say's Elkiss. Elkiss, how are you? I'm doing pretty well, pretty well, said Hilary. After seeing Elkiss it felt like everything in my world was perfect because, she is the best friend anyone could ever have. I got your message, about Jirah not calling you all week. Elkiss had told Hilary. Oh, yeah about that, replied Hilary. " you need some serious counseling because, your personality is changing, and I am worried about you. Say did you hear that new song by Empress Ann? It's titled

"All I wish is"? It is a tight song; kind of like your situation, said Elkiss.

No, I have not been listening to the radio lately, replied Hilary. OMG, you are so like missing out. Maybe we can hang out for like two hours listen to music, and chill out dude, said Elkiss. I'd like that, Hilary had said. How about tonight? And, we can get like an hour of study in too.

Because, I have a big pop quiz on Friday, and I've got to do the best that I can, Hilary explain; while changing into her swim suit. " That is all we can do is our best, like swimming laps". Oh, yeah, and I'm getting her new album too. We can both purchase Empress Ann's album tonight online said Hilary. I was going to buy her album, and we can um, download it on the computer then I can make you a CD, said Elkiss.

Hua? What am I hearing this, Elkiss Empress Ann has the tightest album covers, and we are not poor, only poor people do that. And besides, I am a Fan too. "come on", Elkiss said excitedly, let's go swimming. " They both skipped out speed walking to the pool, and jump laughing up a breeze, just being happy and peaceful students". " girls, girls, said Coach before he could say anything else Hilary, and Elkiss was already in the in the air diving into the pool. Some people laughed, and some people were furious. While Hilary, and Elkiss pulled themselves out of the pool some guy and girl was standing looking at them. And, the guy said, "hey, you see that girl right there??, she has a Hit on her." Elkiss, what is a hit?

Asked Hilary. Where, did you here that from? Asked elkiss. That guy over there pointed towards us, and said that, that girl right there has a hit on her". Explained Hilary. Really? Said Elkiss. Yes, said Hilary. That's scary

Elkiss, what does that mean? It mean somebody paid a bad person to terminate another person, said Elikss. Oh my God... oh my God.. Hilary said. For reals you did not know what that word meant? Out of all smart people you should know, Elkiss had said. Well, I do not, and those people need to go to jail they're worthless. See people like us we're making a difference in the world because, of our actions, those people won't they will just ruin it all. Said Hilary. " Class gather up, say's Coach, today I am doing a timing for eight laps, to see who has strong lungs. If any of you smoke that pot, weed, smoking period you must stop immediately; if you do not stop smoking I will drop you from my class, I need strong lungs not weak lungs. Everyone in position? Ready? Say's the coach,and the whistle blows. Eight laps you are timed. " don't be thinking about you loser boyfriend, you need to focus, said Elkiss. Diving into the water, swimming up Hilary started to swim her laps, and started to think. Swimming, and swimming. Finally, Elkiss, and Hilary had finished. "You should do that all the time girls, says the coach. Whenever, we have days only doing laps, and you are not being timed, take your time then you will have know worries of what to do during the rest of the class. Well, class is just about over, you are all dismissed". Are you going over you boyfriends house today? Asked some girl walking by. What? Replied, Hilary. Oh, don't mind me it's just that " Hilary's Daily News"... travels pretty fast on campus. Do you need advice? No take you time I am in know hurry for you answer. " do I know you? Ask Hilary" "getting Annoyed" Hum... she say's, I will see you next week. We may talk more than."walking away she said, " Do you love me at least for right now" singing. "She think she knows everything, don't pay her any attention", said, Elkiss you must spend the night Empress Ann's song is off the chain. "Okay, okay I will let my mother know, and just come by like around 6:30 pm to pick me up", said Hilary. " Oh, baby, you know I'll be there, said Elkiss, smiling.

Would you like a ride home? Asked Elkiss; I'm giving you a ride home, and I am demanding you to except the ride. You are excepting this ride, and no is not an option. Then when you get home safely and at a timely manner without wasting your time on Dennis, you will relax get you clothes, and study book for Anatomy, and what not and love you. Love yourself again for once",. Said Elkiss. You have a good point their, said Hilary. And, on our way to your house we can listen to a song or two; Elkiss had said. Sounds good to me, ok then I'll see you by the theater in like two hours, my last class is Math, said Hilary. Alright see you then "keep it trigg" the both laughed. I am going to the counseling office I have work study, then math said Hilary. " I know what you meant" said Elkiss. "Hilary? You here good, today you will be alphabetizing all files, and going runs to the mail department.

Graduation is in a couple days so, their are some supplies that is needed you, and Bryson can take to the theater in the back. Alright, Explained Miss. Away. Would you like overtime today? Miss. Away asked no thank you I have another class then I have to study for my Anatomy test today, and evening,and for an hour in the morning. " wait, is tomorrow Thursday, or Friday? Thursday, "oh okay. Oh, okay", said Hilary. My test is on Friday morning but, I must study to keep my grade up so I won't be jeopardized me being on the tennis team, Hilary explained. " I will take the over time, said Bryson". Great settled then. "I am so excited, Miss. Away ", said .Hilary, went over to the file cabinet and started her work. Hum, hum, hum...

B, C, E, A, B, C, D; dang this is a lot of files E. " I have the cart, mail cart full with the graduation supplies, say's Bryson you want to come? He asked Hilary. Yes, " when Hilary began to step up onto her feet Bryson helped her up." Thank you, said Hilary. We'll be back, we must deliver these supplies to the theater for the graduation next week. "Okay, see ya" said another work mate. Wow, by the time we get back it will be time to go; good thing I did those files back words, it was a lot but, I finished my work", said Hilary.

It is always cold in this theater, said Bryson. I know hua said Hilary.

Do you have another class after this? Asked Bryson. Um, why? Said Hilary. Just wanted to start a conversation bryson said. Ahh, yeah I guess Hilary say's. Wait for me said Bryson running catching up to Hilary on there way back to the counseling center. Hilary! Hilary! Yelled Elkiss, you want to go early so we can study for that Anatomy test Friday? I was thinking the same thing, say's Hilary. " know wonder we are best friends, come on", said Elkiss. Getting into the car Elkiss put's on the new CD by " Empress Ann " this song is so tight you have got to here this one first.

" All I Wish Is"

"Yes, I'm that young beautiful girl that will rock your world, I can tell you again, and again loving you ain't nothing. Take heart be smart let's change the world; take my heart,and be smart let me be your girl. My parents wouldn't mind you being my Valentine as long as your only mine all mine; keep those pretty eyes on me babe an watch how people behave ain't nobody really feeling the same as me. Just by talking to you

I felt so, so lucky; my words can not even express even if I never have you, in my mind your always going to be the best, you looking so handsome in your suit, and vest. Even if I only had one hour to spend with you the whole world would move slow except for me and you. If I was able to give you something you already don't have, it would be a gift in a box with know reasons to be mad. When I first set my eyes on you I didn't know what to think except that you needed to hear this from me.

With my whole soul, loyalty, and honesty, when you get ready I think that you should marry me. Not only because, I think the world of you, not only because, I'll pass up anybody except for you until you reject it; ain't nobody feeling the same as me because, as I change the whole world is going to change with me.

When you love somebody your suppose to feel happiness, and joy because, finding love in this world today is fading away.

All I wish is, for one thousand wishes...

All I wish is for one thousand wishes...

All I wish is for one thousand wishes...

All I wish is for one thousand wishes...

All I wish is for one thousand wishes..

I graduated from high school know I'm in college want to know something about me I love knowledge. When I dream my goal is to make it come true; you can't just sit there and think your dreams will come to you. That's how I felt baby, when

I seen you, you took my breathe away had to take a class of psychology. It feels like I'm going crazy knowing you don't love me, lied to my face, and put another above me. you took my love for-granted, now you wish you had this, your mouth nothing but, madness in my eyes was sadness. You could care less about me saying you couldn't do without me, I knew you was nothing but a two way stream, and know that our relationship is so fing through I hope that you can cope on your own. I'm going to pray to god for you, even though your nothing but, a two way stream, you know you was wrong breaking my heart in conclusion of this song, I hope that nothing in your life or mine go wrong. I'm a big girl of course I can be strong, I'm not gone cry. You should have kept it real A, what's the big deal.. ooooo...

They laughing and joking when you know you really love him but, he's nothing but, a two way stream. And, know just when it hit me I know your going to miss me. Miss me, miss me, miss, miss, miss me..

All I wish is for one thousand wishes...

All I wish is for one thousand wishes...

All I wish is for one thousand wishes"...

Dang!.... I am like feeling that on a serious tip said Hilary. "Okay, girl you feel me this is some real like crazy life and death stuff not infatuation but, true love", say's Elkiss". "They said that Empress Ann's life story is in all her songs, like everything that she sings about really happen. But, know one can research her story because, it's classified. You want to know what makes her being an artist so exciting?" Asked Elkiss.

What? Said Hilary. Because, know one wanted to see her get rich, nobody wanted to see her be smart, everybody was jealous, and she never did a damn thing. She's so talented, and beautiful.

This next song is titled " Right Now" this song is even tighter. Wow, she is in like a love battle, said Hilary. yes, I know said, Elkiss. You are absolutely right, I love these songs they're hot Hilary say's. You can listen to music, and study right? Sometimes, what? You wanted to study and listen to music? Asked Hilary. Yeah, said Elkiss, oh, okay well, how about having the music down low, and when we take a break we can turn up the volume? Sounds good to me.

"Right Now"

Baby roll down the windows turn up that A/C I love to fill that lovely ocean breeze.

Baby do you love me, I'm asking do you love me for right now? Turn off the engine let's walk on the beach there is no other place that I'd rather be than here with you. This time we will cherish, this is our world, I will always be your girl. Do you remember the first day we met? No matter what I have no regrets.

Darling do you love me? I'm asking do you love me at least for right now? This sea breeze feels so good to me, baby hold me, baby love me,

I'm asking do you.. love me at least for right now? Do you believe that 24 hours is in one day? When the first hour starts at midnight, where is the other hour? Would you dis me? I'm asking do you love me? At least for right now?

Baby do you love me? I'm asking do you love me at least for right now/ do you want me to want you?

Do you love me like I love you too baby.

I do not want to fornicate, I just want you to marry me, oh baby!! do you love me?

I'm asking do you, love me at least for right now?

La, la, la, la,... just..just... just, for right now. Yeah....

Dang, that's "sad" said Hilary. Yeah, I know would you stop saying that?

Asked Elikss. No, I'm just saying if you listen to the words, it's brilliant, because, she sings as if she's going to...said Hilary. "I know don't say it" said, elkiss. Covering up Hilary's mouth. That's why nobody don't want you to be with Dennis, that heartless son of a; aauuu.... he don't care about you

Hilary, I know it hurts now assuming but, later it will hurt worse because, then it will be a sure thing. Explained Elkiss. "Thank you for your concern but, I love Dennis he'll come around he just need a little time that's all",

Say's Hilary. Hum, it's your heart why do you think heart surgery is so expensive? Asked Elkiss. "Elkiss!" shouted her mom. Yeah! Said Elkiss.

"Oh, hey girls didn't here you come in". Hi Mrs. Ville, how are you today? Asked Hilary. (politely) I am even doing better now that you asked; if you girls need me I'll be planting in my beautiful garden. "Okay mommie," replied Elkiss. Alrighty, let's get to the real loving in deez books. Said

Hilary. "laughing". Know that's the spirit, Elkiss said with a smile. " studying for hours, Hilary's phone rang". I thought you put that phone on vibrate, said Elkiss. Well, what if Dennis calls, and look it is Dennis. Hello, answered Hilary. " how are you doing baby? Said Dennis. It's okay if I call you baby, right/ yes, of course you can call me baby, and I'm doing fine just finish studying for my test on Friday, said Hilary. "Speaking of Friday said Dennis; do you have anything planned? For the night". No, said

Hilary. " would you like to go out on a date with me?" asked Dennis. " I'd love too, said Hilary. Alright, what time do I come pick you up? Say's

Dennis. How about while the sun is setting, said Hilary. Ah, okay I will see you on Friday, said Dennis, bye. Bye, said Hilary. " your going to go out? On a date! Said Elkiss. Come on, don't start with me about my love life, Hilary said. Exactly, love life, fact here you are a virgin, and what if you end up having sex out of wedlock? Said Elkiss. Nothing like that is going to happen, said Hilary. Hum.. well, I don't know you like him like, like him, way to much, and I don't want to see you getting hurt, I'm not trying to make you leave him, just don't give it all away. Do you even understand, what everybody is trying to tell you? Explains Elkiss. Do you even understand what we are trying to prevent? Asked Elkiss. Oh God, you don't because, your blind and if you don't understand because, your blind that can only mean one thing, say's Elkiss. "what"? Said Hilary. That your in love with Dennis. I am in love with him I admit it, I never had feelings like this before; he is my first my last my everything. Hilary said laughing. " No it's not funny, said Elkiss". Whatever happens I will always be here for you, just don't do anything dumb:, said Elkiss. Anything dumb like what? Asked Hilary. " Nothing, come on I'll take you home, elkiss replied.

Okay, oh, hey before I forget meet me in the library in the morning to go over the questions before my test, Hilary said. Okay, sure said Elkiss.

Driving home, Hilary said to Elkiss. Hey, do you think we can get Empress Ann to perform at our graduation? Wouldn't that be the bomb? Replied Elkiss. Yes, oh my god, my mom would be so proud of me, I can see me now walking across the stage getting my degree", said Hilary. Me too but, I'm on your back said Elkiss. And, they both started to laugh. "make sure you call me after your date, she said. Okay, later see you at school tomorrow.

Hi, mom's I'm back home from Elkiss house.

Read: "Hilary, went for a late ride on my bike in the park. Be back in fifteen minutes dinner is in the microwave".

When Hilary began to walk up stairs her mother Liz walked in saying " aren't you going to eat? Before you go to bed." I would like to eat but, I am so tired I had a long day but, my evening made my rest of the day so. Sparkling, peppy, and gay. "That sounds like an amazing feeling, were you jolly, or elated? Asked

Hilary's mom. It was a calm type of happiness pleasant, and content like, replied Hilary. And, let me guess Dennis has something to do with this over whelming joy that you are feeling?" yes, he called me today, said Hilary. " standing up, as Liz walked towards

Hilary, and said; that is good, gave Hilary a hug, and kissed her on her cheek good night sweetie". Good night, replied Hilary, I knew that he was going to come around, my gosh my heart was pounding, so slowly. Hilary thought to herself. Hilary had took a shower, when her cellphone began to ring she expected it to be her best friend Elkiss but, it wasn't it was the man of her dreams Dennis. Hello, Dennis Hilary answered. " how did you know that it was me?" he asked. Oh, I have you on my caller I.D.

Memory. Hilary said, " oh, oh okay well, I was just calling because, I wanted to stop by to kiss you, I know it's kind of late so I will just wait till tomorrow; I just wanted you to know that I was thinking of you, said

Dennis". Really, I always think of you Dennis, I love you so much, say's Hilary. " I'll talk to you tomorrow, call me when you get home from school okay, demanded Dennis. Okay, I love you Dennis, said Hilary. For reals? He asked. Yes, answered

Hilary. "Okay, good night I'll talk to you tomorrow", Dennis said "again". Alright, good night, Hilary said.

Beep, beep, beep, beep....{sound of alarm clock}

Hilary it is 6:30 a.m. "Today is Friday don't you have a big test today in Anatomy?" Asked Liz. No, mom it is tomorrow, Friday. Said Hilary. "ah, no sweetie today is in fact Friday, yesterday was Thursday. Okay, you win said Hilary, yawning. Take a shower said Liz. I took a shower last night, replied Hilary. Or a wash off, and come to the kitchen to eat breakfast.

{ding, Dong} somebody is at the door, it's Elkiss; I was suppose to meet her at the library to quiz me, mom. " I have a car so why wait? Besides

I'll be sitting there waiting for you", say's Elkiss. Well meet me down town then.

I told you a certain time for a reason, said Hilary, okay, I'll meet you down town said Elkiss. Cool bye, said Hilary.

Shortly after Elkiss left from Hilary's house, Hilary left to see Dennis but, as usual Dennis was not there. Hilary had thoughts of Dennis answering the door, and assumed he would be home but, as usual he wasn't.

Well, I'd better get to school she said to herself . Walking into the library What's the matter Hilary? Elkiss asked. " nothing" said Hilary with a smile. Hilary, hi said

Woo. What's up Hilary said charles. " Don't make me over! Hilary we all know that you went to see if Dennis was there at home, said Razzmatazz. And, she started to sing.

"Don't Make Me Over"

Don't make me ova- don't make me ova- don't make me ova because it's youI can't seem to get ova.

Don't make me ova- don't make me ova- don't make me ova because, it's you I can't seem to get ova.

Don't make me ova- don't make me ova- don't make me ova because, it's you I can't seem to get ova.

At first it felt like you was my best friend, you was someone I could talk to all night again and again. What happen to you? Or was it me I can't seem to find the problem that never seemed. Why did you act like you loved me? Where is your humanity? Why is it always men like you, who pick good women like me?

Could it be you getting paid? so desperate to tell lies just to get laid? You Can have any woman but, me you act so over sexed could you possibly Have HIV? I don't ever want to be with you again; after you cheating on Me. You can have any woman you want but, me get away from me you Monsterous human being.

Don't make me ova- don't make me ova- don't make me ova because, it's you I Can't seem to get ova. Don't make me ova- don't make me ova, don't make me Ova because, it's you I can't seem to get ova.

The thought of losing you will never be because, I know deep down inside that You truly love only me. You and me will always be together forever, why would You want it any other way? Not talking, or being together everyday. I love the Sound of your voice the vibe I get from looking into your eyes, there is nothing I'd ever need more but, to be by your side. To me you are pristine especially, When you, hold me, just let me be your one and only. I'm only being Honest about how I feel about you. The decision is up to you.

Don't make me ova, don't make me ova, don't make me ova because, its You I can't seem to get ova.

Don't make me ova, don't make me ova, don't make me ova because, its You I can't seem to get ova..

I will never do anything to hurt you, I will, be there for you. The thought of Losing you, makes my heart freeze. The thought of losing you makes my Heart freeze.. au, baby your touch feels so good to me, I love it when You spend time with me, you and me will always be together.

Don't make me ova, don't make me ova, don't make me ova because, its You I can't seem to get ova. Don't make me ova, don't make me ova, don't Make me ova because, it's you I can't seem to get ova.

If you need a shoulder I am always here for you, if you want a Valentine calling me is all you have to do. Love, and understanding the Whole day through, happiness of you being mine, my lovely valentine. Don't make me ova, don't make me ova, don't make me ova because, it's you I can't seem to get ova. Don't make me ova, don't make me ova, don't Make me ova because, it's you I can't seem to get ova. In my.. in my mind I only see you. Don't make me! Don't make me…. Don't make me ova……

"Kids quiet down, your in the library", said the librarian. If you have a Class you will not regret going. Hilary, and Elkiss walked to class, see you Later.

Alright, Charles, Hilary, and Woo you three are on time; good know all you Need is a Humming bird number 2 pencil put the rest of your belongings Under the chair, you will have sixty minutes to do your test, and do your Best, and remember your athletic coach gets these grades you may begin. Hilary, whispered the professor I've heard about your Love situation please try Your best to concentrate. Okay, said Hilary. You think you passed? Asked Charlee. I did ok,

I studied, I better had passed, said Hilary. So did I, I studied The whole two days said woo. Hey Hilary, you leaving already? Said woo

Yeah, you gone? You not going to hang around for your grade? Said Charlee. Not today, professor can just email me. I know I passed said Hilary. Alright… are you still with that guy Dennis? Asked Charlee. Yes, we are Going out tonight, said Hilary." Oh" said woo that's cool I guess I hope you Have a good time, be safe, said woo. "Yeah, safe', said Charlee. Not knowing What to say alright, see yall next week. "kay bye hilary.

(Knock,knock) who is it?, Hilary, oh my gosh it's his dad; hello sir is Dennis home? "no, he's not here" said Dennis dad. Okay, um can you let Him know that I came by? My name is Hilary. " I know" he said. " laughing" Hilary say's thank you. Since Dennis was not home I went to my granny'sHouse, " hey, grams! How are you doing? " hi baby" said granny. How you Doin? Fine, just came home early from school, I was feeling a little bit low

That is all. I was gong to the movies but, since I skip a class I don't really Feel like going. You need help cleaning up, or with anything? " you can do The rest of the dishes if you want too:, said Granny. That sounds good To me, said Hilary. You cook anything grandma? " I got some left over Duck, granny said". Yum,I want some can you make me some dressing? Pretty please grandmother. " yes, I will make you some for next week just Have your mom to bring you on by to get a plate okay". Yess, thanks Grams, you always make my days better. Grandma?? What was it like in Your day? When you was young? " we use to pick cotton in the cotton Fields. But, it's nothing to learn about, nothing to learn about" said Grandmother.

Just you go to church, or the kingdom Hall she said. Okay grandma. Next Thing you know Hilary had fallen asleep on the couch. When Hilary had Awaken, her mom was there to pick her up. But, before she left she Called Dennis on his cell phone. And, lately he has not been answering,

First for days then weeks. Surprisingly, a couple weeks later he had given her a call to go out on a date, and what a date it was. (phone ringing).

Hello say's Hilary; when she answered the phone. " what you up to baby?" a Soft voice spoke through the telephone. Dennis?, said Hilary. "yes, it's me". He replied. Why haven't you been home? What are you up too? You Haven't called me in like forever, and I went by your house you are never Home. I…I want to be with you. Hilary said to Dennis in a lonely voice. Ok.. Are you at home? Wait, of course you are at home I called you. Ha,ha. How about tonight? I'll come by and we can hang out together. That sounds great she said. " how about I pick you up in like thirty Minutes?", Said Dennis. Yes, I will be ready, I'll be outside waiting for you Like five minutes before. Little did she know that Dennis had a whole Entire different life with someone else. Actually Hilary had know idea Never even cross her mind. The only thoughts she'd ever have was If he thought about ever getting married? Does he have any kids?

What was his favorite color? What kind of food does he like? What Do he think about most? Does he like movies? And, most of all what is He searching for in life? A soul mate? What was he looking for when he Picked me to be with? Beep, beep… with a big smile on her face, she

Open the door to the SUV, lean over to kiss him, then said; are you Happy to see me right now? "Of course I am say's Dennis. So how is Everything at home?" good I am always thinking of you, talking to my Friends about you, said Hilary. " for reals? Crazy dennis said. Other than that I am in college I'm going to finish sooner or later but, I am overall ok. I am not Exspecting my family to love me forever anyway this earth is not paradise. And they both laughed. " this is not paradise" repeated Dennis.

I thought you was going to take me to the movies or something.. out for a nice drink, why are we parked here? In front of your house? Asked Hilary. " I live in Los Angeles but, I live with my parents too, I am only out here for tonight because, I came to see you, and spend time with you for a little bit then I am leaving out of town, " explained Dennis. Oh so, is that what you do is just smoke weed, and work? Asked Hilary. " No, Dennis said.

I attend a University". Oh, cool you can concentrate while you are high? (laughs) " I believe weed is thee most healthy plant for man, I will always smoke weed, I will never stop smoking weed you want to try some? Dennis ask Hilary. Ah, no I don't think I can concentrate like you can, while I am in college "here go ahead he insisted he had kissed her. Dennis has given Hilary a kiss that made her think that she meant the world to him. He lean towards her smiling with his dreamy eyes, and soft voice french kissing her. And that was the last thought she'd ever want to happen.

I feel so warm, am I high/ Hilary thought to herself. Dang.. he likes weed is this what we are going to do all the time when you come spend time with me? wait before you answer that, said Hilary. Then she lean to him and gave him a kiss a real long kiss a kiss that she would not even be able to forget even if she tried.

You know what? It is getting kind of late I better get back home because, I do not have a house key.

I'm sorry Hilary said to Dennis. "What? Baby, you don't have to say sorry I completely understand "said Dennis. Oh, okay.. said Hilary then he started up the car put on his seat belt, and drove to her house. When she was hoping that he'd ask if she wanted to come go with him.

But, he didn't and, from then on Hilary was sad, sad to the point were she knew that she would never be his number one because, she felt that he had someone else, or maybe he was to busy, or maybe he has situations of his own.

"Why are you so quiet? Dennis asked", I don't know said Hilary." I guess, what you not feeling me right now? Said Dennis" we're not together enough, said Hilary. " I really, really like you but, I got to make sure that I got myself straight before I settle down, that's all explained

Dennis". Okay, well thank you for clearing that up but, I did not say anything, if you feel that this is how you want us to be then so be it obviously, it is up to you; now that I know I will just make my steps rare coming asking for you, said Hilary. "You don't have to stop coming over, it's just that I mean I won't be there, Dennis said "laughing". But, you can still come by. I can just call you said Hilary. " That will be great too", said Dennis. Sometimes I will be at school and I can call you on my break, said Hilary. "And, if I don't answer you can leave a message, and I will call you back", ok said

Dennis

Good you was driving slow, I am going to miss you so much, it's best that I keep how I really feel to myself, Hilary told him. " next time you make sure you can stay out later than usual, or you know,

I can pick you up earlier, so we can talk more", said Dennis Really, Hilary said." yes, really good night I'll tak to you later on alright." said Dennis. When Hilary got out of the car she decided to try to forget the time they spent together but, she couldn't their was a space in her heart that was able to hold him right there for later in life.

Remembering someone you truly love, and forgetting what you put in that little spot in your heart for later can truly be damaging. It has painful side effects that everyone in life experiances with the saying.

" There's something missing in my life but, I don't know what it is, or I have everything I want yet, I still feel so incomplete". Have you ever had that feeling before? Have you ever said any of those words?

And, what is so sad love can come at a very young age. Some people live their whole lives feeling so empty. Even after marriage because, they have already found a love either when they was little, or at teen years. Sometimes it could be like somebody is calling you in the air, spirit, in dreams, or imagining someone but, you do not know who it is because, someone is in love with you. Love is an emotion that can take you over, make you over if you let it. Being in love can also lead to death, give happiness, or being in loneliness for the rest of your life. But, if you have willpower you can just label love as being the dumbest word, and try your best to move on in your life. Even though you feel hopeless their is an entire world to see, and it is better to see the world instead of making mistakes, or putting yourself in a situation that seems impossible to get out of.

Because, sooner or later you will realize that the love that you can express, and the intense love that you can have for another human being is not in every person on this earth. Some men, and women that do love each other cheats because, they are weak, end up breaking up, and making up because, their confused or end up killing each other. Is, or isn't that love? Having an attitude of " if I can not have you then know one can"... word has it that, if you truly love that person you'd want the best for him, or her. Which is very true but, it is not true that if you let him go, and if he comes back to you than it is true love.

That's not true, why let someone go when you have there life in your hands? Do you think that a person who say's that they are "in love" would not commit suicide over the person that they are in love with should be considered crazy?

Some men, and women rather die than to be without the one their heart, mind, body, and soul loves. Sometimes, the lucky person that is loved dearly excepts it. Sometimes, the lucky person that is loved dearly rejects it. Love nowadays has to be treated as a battle field.

With the numbers of love cooling off many hearts will be broken, many lives will be ruin, but most of all in this world when love fails people will know longer love each other. Mankind will look at life with no value. Life is valueless, baby? Who wants babies? Who cares?

You ain't nobody to me; live today die tomorrow, die today no worries tomorrow. I want to be free from it all. My moto is with know love their is know peace, and with know peace their is know compassion for life in general.

Love is dangerous especially being in it, you must know what you are doing, when you say " that you are in love with a man, or a woman" because, if you are not emotionally ready to handle love, then you have no business being in love period. However, everyone has their own opinion.

I believe when someone is in love, and it is rejected that he, or she can become something in life. Using that passion, using that energy towards something else you have always wanted. From fame, to be educated will not fail. Because, it wont reject your love, and passion you have for it.

{knock at the door...it's me..}

" Hilary if you keep on coming inside at this time of night I am not going to open the door. It is way to late to be coming in at this time of night understand? And, keep on messing with these men, your going to end up getting someone you can not get rid of", said Hilary's mom. Okay, mom sorry for coming in late and, I know I am not messing with nobody who is crazy about me. I'm not that pretty, I just need someone to talk too. Besides, I'm in school, and I don't want nothing to get in the way of me getting my education. It's not like he will give me the things I want and, need. " well, there is some diner in their left over if you are hungry", said Liz Hilary's mom. Thanks said Hilary.

I need to get some rest I have a big test tomorrow, and I have not had any sleep all day, said Hilary. " before you go to bed take a shower you smell like smoke",

Liz said. Oh, sorry mom said Hilary. "No, you better not be smoking, and doing drugs if you want to get kicked out then keep on doing it" said Liz. I was not smoking it was Dennis he smokes mom, explained Hilary. " oh, okay I was just letting you know", said Liz

Alright mom good night I'm a sleepy head now, said Hilary. When hilary took a shower it was very warm, wetting her hair washing towards her face the water felt really good. Fantasizing about Dennis, Hilary goes into a daze.

"kissing, oh so passionately Dennis rubs, and touches Hilary on her bottom rubbing his hands, and caressing her back. French kissing her like never before, never feeling a kiss so amazing in her life. She shivers, and say's "oohhh" with such a soft voice. Dennis penetration felt so deadly to Hilary, he slowly, and softly laid her on the bed, put his hands around her and gently pulled her hair; then pressed pressure upon her body. Hilary, wanted to tell Dennis how much she loved him but, the words just couldn't come out, eyes watery.

As the wetness became, a river of tears. Between their bodies becoming one together in a moonlight of passionate love. Know one will never take my love from me, know one will never know what true love we have she felt those emotions in her heart. Dennis had took Hilary by the hands, and held them, and pushed her legs wide open. In that moment she knew that Dennis had took everything from her. Love that she didn't know that she even had let alone a heart that wouldn't be able to take the pain if he ever decided to leave. Falling asleep in her bed in her fantasy of making passionate love to Dennis, he fell asleep with his arms around her, and his self inside her deepest secrets".

" Hilary wake up, Hilary wake up you are going to be late if you sleep for another thirty minutes. Don't you have an extra class today?

Asked Liz. No, mom that was yesterday, I go to tennis, and I go tomorrow morning. "Oh, yes that's right sorry I forgot. I made some breakfast would you like to come and eat? Said Liz. What are we having? Asked Hilary. " sausage, eggs, and toast with anything to drink", said Liz. Sounds good, mom okay I'll be down give me like five minutes, said Hilary. After, Hilary brushed her teeth, and washed her face she made her way down stairs into the kitchen table to eat breakfast.

"Are you going to school today?, Hilary's mom had asked. Of course, but, I am going to two classes today instead of four, I was going to go with grandma to Las Vegas, NV if that is okay with you? She was mentioning going the other day so I was hoping this could be my first time traveling out of California. School is about

to be out for spring break said Hilary. " oh, you get vacations? Said Liz" . Yes, I am in college mom, said Hilary. " if your grandmother say's that you can go than, you may go, said Liz I will be going over to her house tomorrow afternoon so, you can just go to your grandmother's house after school tomorrow".

Okay sounds like a good idea, said Hilary. Yum, this is so good," so what's on your agenda for this morning? After eating your breakfast?, asked Liz.

I am going to clean up the bathroom, vacuum the hallway, and the living room, said Hilary. Is that why you woke me up so early mom?

No, I thought you had an early class honest, said Liz, with a laugh.

I'm going to buy you a special alarm clock that will wake you up on the days you need to be up early, and the days you do not need to be up early. You know what that means? Said Hilary's mom. Really, that would be real nice I forgot all about buying an alarm clock said

Hilary. " did you take a shower or a wash off" asked Hilary's mom. I took a wash off because, I get real sensitive in the morning hours, I took a real long shower last night anyway because, I was around all that smoke with Dennis and, besides I have great hygiene; is their anymore sausage? Hilary asked her mother. " yes, I made two each she said, ok well, I am going to eat this last one, and I am going to clean up. After that, I will be catching the bus to school.

" I need to go to a few places to take care of some business so I will see you later", said Liz. What time is it mom? "It is 8:27 a.m." Liz said.

Okay, thanks mom. Hilary saw her mom to the door, and as soon as she pulled out the drive way Hilary went to the telephone, and called Dennis to see if he'd answer the phone for once.

While the phone had rang on the other line of the phone, Hilary started to clean up the house. From one end to the other the phone rang and just rang he never answered. Well, what can I expect out of some druggie? Finally getting finished with chores Hilary was on her way off to school for her second, and third class, walking up the street in sight is two cars in a terrible wreck, and one of the cars was upside down in the middle of the street. " oh, my god" somebody died Hilary whispered to herself. The ambulance, and fire fighters look like they was trying their best to help the people but, they seemed like they were already gone.

" the bus stops here are closed here, you'll have to walk up the street a fire fighter had said to Hilary". This morning seemed so strange to

Hilary it felt like she had dreamed of a day like today before but, she just could not remember who was driving and what had happen in her dreams. Getting to school today it is going to be a smooth, and peaceful day for me, Hilary said to herself. When she went to the girls locker room changing in her red swim suit, she over heard two other girls talking about their boyfriends. Sorry to interrupt, but, what does it mean when your boyfriend never answers his phone? Hilary asked.

And, when he does he acts strange, and hardly wants to spend time with you? " First of all you need to think about it, what else could he be doing if he see's your number, and presses decline each and every time you call? No doubt he is being with someone else. Maybe he works, and goes to school but, still their should not be anything that can come between you two, know mater how busy you both are. If he fails to call you today, and it is a Wednesday! He doesn't care about you move on before you get torn apart. Trust me I know these things there are way better looking men and a whole world you have not seen yet. Don't be in such a rush to give your heart away. Hilary is it?" yes, how did you know? Said Hilary "your in tennis right? She asked well, I take the same class too." oh, cool, what's your name? Asked

Hilary. " Kitasha" as you were saying. " my major is Marriage, and relationship in

Psychology. You don't need it now and if you decide to wait statistics are that you will feel worse in the future, if you let him treat you like this now it becomes worse because, he truly cares less." said Kitasha. How do you know? Asked Hilary. "this is my second year and after preqs I chose to do the most important subjects first, you do not want to be a victim of mistaking love, you must understand for your good that love is a heart felt emotion that only feels compassion, caring it doesn't think about rejection and that's what it sounds like, it's headed first he ignores your calls, does not call back. What else does he do? Said Kitasha" I get your point talk with you later said Hilary." I don't mean to be rude about this and I know it is none of my business get it through your head " he does not love you" as she held Hilary by the shoulders, if he is willing to waste his time driving for 2 hours, no sex, no oral sex, but, gets you high as a kite to where you are unaware of your surroundings. You trust that man with your very life.

Now, if you ask me that is something to lose if you ain't got nothing.

"While the group of girls was walking out towards the pool" he's either a hit man, a murder, or somebody is paying him some good money to watch you. Said Kitasha.

" you girls! Come here! Yelled, the swimming coach, you almost got marked

absent. Only ten laps today, you will be timed". After the ten laps what do we do? Asked Hilary " looking at the size of the pool and it is an Olympic size, so it should take you half the time of class remember this is not a race. If you just so happen to finish before your classmates you may use the extra time as free time" said coach. Diving into the swimming pool Hilary felt lost she did not know what was to come of her relationship, or was it even a relationship.

Swimming, and swimming kitasha swam pass Hilary saying

"stop crying, and suck it up sick puppy" She said.

Stopping an holding herself up above water Hilary's mind was blanked out. What if she is right? What if he does not love me? What if he is hiding something from me? But, what could I have done to anyone for something like this to happen to me? " Hilary! Enough showing off not everyone can do that. Continue".

Breathing heavily, with her orange swim goggles dipping in and out of the water, bathing suit fitted so perfectly. Finishing up kitasha say's

"I'm sorry, I'm sorry... it's just that girls think of hurting themselves over men, and you are so pretty, and young you have a whole life ahead of you it just wouldn't be fair. For your future, forget him okay." come on you can walk with me, Hilary said laughing; you act like this is a dangerous situation. " it is, Kitasha said. So

what are you doing for the rest of the day?" I am going to see my fam bam, said Hilary

"sounds fun" changing her clothes, I am so glad that I do not have another class after this, I feel so navy blueish. " you just started dating him right?" asked Kitasha. Yes." And, so far it is okay? Kitasha said. I guess. "Well, never be afraid to run maybe the best thing you could do, for yourself said, Kitasha. Now, why would I do that? Because, if he is not ashamed, then why should you be? See you later kay... bye waiting on the bus Hilary started to think to herself, just take it a day at a time I am thin, pretty, and smart what could possible go wrong? It can't be me. The bus arrived, and Hilary step into the bus, and sat down. Another day of watching people, I can't wait until this class is over psychology one page today. I see a young woman, and her children she has a little toddler boy, and a little girl . Her age seems to be a teenager not to well dressed, looks like she is struggling alone.

With her kids, might have a job I also see an old man he always runs when he get's onto the bus; like he was wishing that he was child again.

He is wearing a Kangol hat, and nice pants, he smiles. Each an every time I take this route the bus goes by Dennis house. Well, this is my stop thank you have a nice day. Walking down the street their was really nothing else Hilary could think about, only him. The man that took control of her soul. Dang... this doesn't feel right I have got to do something about this maybe grandmother will know what to do.

Oh, cool mom is there, aw man now I can't ask her what to do...

"Hilary wants to go out of state with you, and I told her she could go but, it was up to you" said Liz. I heard that, who said my name?

"everyone started to laugh". Hi, grams hi mom said Hilary. " how was class today? Asked Liz" swimming. Swimming? It was highly enlightening classmates had lots to say about it all, you know getting older girl type stuff, just things you wish never existed. " you want to go out of state with me?, I won't be out there long, said Grandmother." where are you going anyway? Asked Hilary. "Las Vegas" Las Vegas?

Is it nice out there? Hilary asked. " oh, yes granny said, you will love it". So can I go? " yes, you can go said Liz". So when will you be leaving?, so that I can be ready. " after you get out of school and get on your vacation, said Grandmother. Oh, that is perfect, said Hilary.

"how is your man friend? Said grandmother. Oh Dennis? He is okay I guess.

" Another reason I am letting you come with me is because, I don't think you should be with that man, he's no good for you, grandmother said. How can you be so sure, grandmother? You have not even met him yet, Said Hilary. " well, from how your mom makes it sound we don't think that he is right for you, said Hilary's grandmother.

"oh, have you had sex with him yet? Asked Liz". Well umm... " sit down! In a demanding voice as her mother pulled up a chair". The reason why we ask is because, we are concerned, that he does not pass an STD on to you; you know what a Sexually Transmitted

Disease is right? You pay attention in class?" yes, mom why? Dang.. yelled Hilary. " No!, you listen to me you live with all of us, we eat out of the same damn dishes, we use the same washing machine, same shower. All of that and, you need to be careful, and not sleep around. now, you should know better than to be a stupid girl thinking everybody likes you. You know that boy only wants one thing, fresh meat between your legs; if you have already gave it up it is bound to come to an end, I just don't understand Hil. I thought you were smarter than that, I am upset with you; you need to go on this small trip, and the family needs to think if you should continue. In the mean time go to the doctor, and get tested for HIV, Syphilis, Chlamydia, and all that, and get birth control too". Said Liz .

As Hilary walked out crying, her mother said " go to the clinic". Okay, I will is that it? That's all you wanted to talk to me about? Said Hilary. Ah, let me think yes", liz said. Cool, I am going home said Hilary. " your going to ride with me, said Liz". No, I want to catch the bus, I need to be alone for awhile see you at home mom ok, said Hilary.

"walking back to the bus stop Hilary felt even more scared than ever it seem like everyone knows something that I don't; as she entered onto the bus she notices a guy that was still on the bus. The bus went into a big circle, now it feels like I am being followed.

I'll be able to know if he gets onto the same bus Hilary said to herself. This is my stop, I pushed the button, Hilary yelled. " sorry about that, here you go said the bus driver".

Dang, now that guy know which stop I get off at, and out of the blue there he was walking right behind her. Maybe he is visiting somebody around here Hilary thought to herself. So she walked across the street, then he walked across the street too. Hey, are you following me? Hilary asked the stranger. Yes, I am I wanted to know where you live? And do you have a boyfriend? He explained.. you sick-o! Get the hell away from me before I scream, Hilary yelled out loud; get away! Somebody help! HELP!!! " okay, okay I'll go sorry, said the stranger". Hilary waited at the corner, and made sure that he was out of sight, and ran home. Busting through the door she rushes to the telephone, and started to talk to herself saying," now if he does not answer then sex is all he is waiting for, please don't let them be right please... dailing the number, the telephone began to ring...ring...ringing.. and ringing..

No.. said Hilary.. " I am going to let you in on a secret, I might have to tell you this again, said Liz".

" I remember when I first fell in love, I did not know what to think it was real. But, the way I felt after he left me, still has not left my heart, or stomach till this very day. When he'd come into my mind of me thinking of him; he was not only my sweetheart, the passion I'd feel..it..it. Finally, felt like I understood what Jesus Christ meant by having passion. Only God could mold you to feel such deep affection for another human being. And, when we made love I was so overwhelmed, the power he had with just a touch. The smell of his hair, the taste of his lips, with his beautiful eyes looking into mine, looking steadily, and intensely

asif he was getting curious", said Liz. " my point is" as she went on, don't love him so deeply.

"Are you packed for in the morning? " Said Liz. Yes, I just need to put a couple more things in my bag said Hilary. " Are you excited?

Liz asked". Excited?, of course first time leaving out of California to Las Vegas, Nevada hopefully it is as exciting as it sounds. " ha, indeed it is young women your age loves it out in Las Vegas, don't get lost, don't run off, and remember you are there to visit your family". Said Liz

How long does it take to get out there on the bus? Asked Hilary. " It's a round trip but,, not that long around two hours, it also depends on the driver, how many stop or breaks, and people. I think you should leave four hours before dawn because, at night is when everything is glamorous said Liz". Oh, my goodness mom, may I stay out there if I like it?

Hilary asked. " what about Dennis? And college? And your friends?",

Said Liz. Well, ah I will think it over, said Hilary. " okay, it is getting late we both need to get some rest, we've had a long day today, said

Liz" okay. Mom said Hilary. Good night, I love you.

I love you too.

To Be Continued...

Printed in the United States
By Bookmasters